This Center Point Large Print edition
is published in the year 2001 by arrangement with
Golden West Literary Agency.

The text of this Large Print edition is unabridged.
In other aspects, this book may vary from the original
edition. Printed in Thailand. Set in 16-point Plantin type by
Bill Coskrey.

ISBN 1-58547-080-5

Library of Congress Cataloging-in-Publication Data

Le May, Alan, 1899-1964.
    The searchers / Alan Le May.-- Center Point large print ed.
    p. cm.
    ISBN 1-58547-080-5 (lib. bdg. : alk. paper)
    1. Large type books. I. Title.

PS3523.E513 S4 2001
813'.52--dc21

00-050911